THOMAS & FRIENDS™

Thomas and Bertie's Race

Based on
The Railway Series
by the
Rev. W. Awdry

Illustrations by
Robin Davies

EGMONT

EGMONT

We bring stories to life

First published in Great Britain in 2017
by Egmont UK Limited
The Yellow Building, 1 Nicholas Road, London W11 4AN

Thomas the Tank Engine & Friends™

CREATED BY BRITT ALLCROFT

HiT entertainment

ISBN 978 1 4052 8576 6
66191/1
Printed in Italy

Written by Emily Stead. Designed by Claire Yeo.
Series designed by Martin Aggett.

FSC
MIX
Paper
FSC® C018306

Egmont is passionate about helping to preserve the world's remaining ancient forests.
We only use paper from legal and sustainable forest sources.

This book is made from paper certified by the Forestry Stewardship Council® (FSC®),
an organisation dedicated to promoting responsible management of forest resources.
For more information on the FSC, please visit www.fsc.org. To learn more about Egmont's
sustainable paper policy, please visit www.egmont.co.uk/ethical

*When a bus called Bertie
came to my station one day,
he thought he was faster than me!
We decided to have a race to
see whose wheels could
roll the quickest . . .*

Thomas was waiting at a station one day, when a bus pulled up next to him.

"Hello," said Thomas. "Who are you?"

"I'm Bertie. Who are you?"

"I'm Thomas, I run this Branch Line."

"I took your passengers when you were stuck in the snow," said Bertie. "I've come to help today."

"I don't need help from a **slowcoach** like you," huffed Thomas.

"Slowcoach?" Bertie gasped. "I'll race you."

They lined up together.

"Ready, steady . . . **Go!**" said the Stationmaster.

And they were off!

Thomas started slowly, as Bertie zoomed ahead. But Thomas didn't hurry.

"Why don't you go **fast**? Why don't you go **fast**?" Annie and Clarabel worried.

"Wait and see! Wait and see!" smiled Thomas.

"He's a long way ahead!" cried Clarabel.

Thomas had remembered the level crossing.

The crossing gates were down. Bertie had to wait, while Thomas and his carriages steamed through.

"Goodbye, Bertie!" Thomas called.

Then the road left the railway, and Thomas couldn't see Bertie. He had to stop at a station to let some passengers off the train.

"**Peep! Peep!** Quickly, please!" Thomas whistled.

Everybody got out, the Guard blew his whistle, and off Thomas steamed.

"Come along! Come along!" puffed Thomas.

"We're coming along! We're coming along!" sang Annie and Clarabel.

Then Thomas saw Bertie, crossing the bridge over the railway.

"Toot! Toot!" beeped Bertie.

"Steady, Thomas," said his Driver.

"We'll beat Bertie yet. We'll beat Bertie yet," Thomas' carriages called.

But there was a station ahead. As Thomas puffed in, he heard another **"Toot! Toot!"**

"You must be tired, Thomas," Bertie teased. "I can't stop. **Goodbye!**"

Thomas reached the next station quickly,
but he had to wait at a signal.

"Cinders and ashes!" he cried.

He had a drink of water and felt much better.
Then the signal dropped.

"Peep! Peep! We're off!" Thomas whistled.

Thomas smiled, as he crossed the bridge.
Below was Bertie, stopped at a red traffic light.

But the lights soon changed to green, and Bertie
raced after Thomas. **"Brmm! Brmm!"**

Thomas whooshed into the last station at full speed. Bertie rolled in just behind.

"We've won the race! **Hooray**!" Thomas smiled.

His passengers cheered and clapped.

"Well done, Thomas," said Bertie. "That was **fun**, but you were too **fast** for me!"

Thomas and Bertie are now good friends. Together, they take passengers all over Sodor.

The Fat Controller has told Thomas not to race at dangerous speeds, and Bertie's passengers don't like being bounced around like peas in a pan.

Thomas and Bertie would love to have another race, but I don't think they ever will. Do you?

More about Bertie

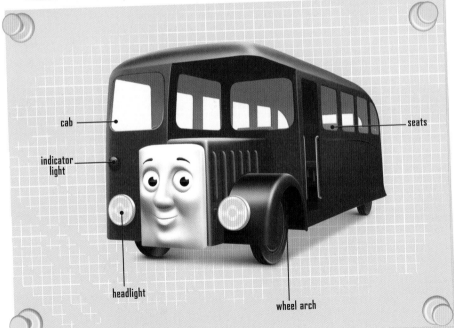

cab

seats

indicator light

headlight

wheel arch

Bertie's challenge to you

Look back through the pages of this book
and see if you can spot:

car

signal

cows

traffic lights

passengers